ZPL

Bubble-Gum Radar

Text and jacket art by
Rosemary Wells

Interior illustrations by
Jody Wheeler

VOLO

Hyperion Books for Children
New York

Volo and the Volo colophon are trademarks of Disney Enterprises, Inc.

Printed in the United States of America

First Edition
1 3 5 7 9 10 8 6 4 2

Library of Congress Cataloging-in-Publication Data on file.
ISBN 0-7868-0722-9 (hc)
ISBN 0-7868-1528-0 (pbk.)

Visit www.hyperionchildrensbooks.com

"It's Square–Dance Day!"

said Mrs. Jenkins.

"Hooray!" shouted everyone.

"Hooray!" shouted the Franks,

louder than everyone else.

The Franks spit their bubble gum
into the air over Nora's head. It
came down and hit her in the ear.
"Ouch!" yelled Nora.
"We were just playing around,"
said the Franks.

Mrs. Jenkins did not even turn

from the blackboard.

"My bubble-gum radar is beeping!"

she said.

"Please take the gum out.

No gum in school!"

"Timothy, would you like to

come up?" asked Mrs. Jenkins.

"Please draw the class a square."

Timothy went to the blackboard.

He drew a triangle.

Then he sat down.

"That's a wonderful triangle,
Timothy," said Mrs. Jenkins.
"One more side, and it's a square.
Try again, Timothy."
Timothy tried to get up from his
seat. He was stuck.

There was a big piece of pink
bubble gum on Timothy's chair.
"Who put the gum on Timothy's
seat?" asked Mrs. Jenkins.
No one answered.

"My bubble-gum radar tells me

it might be someone whose name

is Frank," said Mrs. Jenkins.

"We were just kidding," said

one Frank.

"We didn't know he'd sit down

on it," said the other Frank.

"The gum goes in the wastebasket," said Mrs. Jenkins. "All of it, please. Doris, will you come up and show the class how many corners there are in a square?" asked Mrs. Jenkins.

Doris went to the board. Doris
tried to decide where the corners
of the square were. Then she
thwacked her big tail on the floor.

At that moment, both Franks began to make rude noises with their hands under their armpits. "That will be enough, Franks," said Mrs. Jenkins.

In science class, Fritz was ready to show his experiment.

He poured baking soda into the cone of his volcano.

"You think you are so smart!" said one of the Franks.

He pushed Fritz's volcano.

The volcano fell over.

"Be careful, please!" cried Fritz.

"Now I have to put the volcano together all over again."

"Just kidding!" said Frank.

"I think Frank will have to wait in the quiet corner for a while," said Mrs. Jenkins.
Frank had to sit in the quiet corner during playtime.

On the playground, the other

Frank ran for a football pass.

"Get out of my way!" he shouted.

Nora was playing hopscotch.

Frank banged right into Nora.

He did not say he was sorry.

Instead he said, "Just kidding!"

Yoko helped Nora up.

"You have a nosebleed," said Yoko.

"I will take you to the school

nurse."

The school nurse asked Nora to

lie down. She put an ice pack on

Nora's nose.

"You'll feel better right away,

Nora," she said.

"Did somebody bump into you?"

she asked.

Nora and Yoko were quiet.

"I bet it was one of those

Franks," said the school nurse.

Mrs. Jenkins had seen everything through the classroom window. When playtime was over, both Franks were sitting in the quiet corner.

"Now, do you think you can eat lunch without bothering anybody else?" asked Mrs. Jenkins.

"Oh, sure!" said one Frank.

"We were just kidding, anyway," said the other Frank.

But during lunchtime, when
Mrs. Jenkins was not looking, one
Frank sat on Claude's sandwich.
The other Frank squirted Doris's
squeeze cheese out the window.
"We were just kidding!" they said
to Doris and Claude.

"It's square-dance practice time!"

said Mrs. Jenkins.

"I want everybody to pick their

partner."

Yoko picked Timothy.

Charles picked Nora.

Grace picked Claude.

Doris picked Fritz.

But no one picked the Franks.

"No fair!" the Franks complained.

"No fun!"

"Well, you can't square-dance

without a partner,"

said Mrs. Jenkins.

"But nobody picked us!"

said the Franks.

"You can pick each other!" said

Mrs. Jenkins.

"No way am I going to pick

him!" said one Frank.

"Why not?" asked Mrs. Jenkins.

"He sneezes on me and steps on
my feet," said one Frank.

"He pushes!" said the other Frank.

"And he pops his gum."

"And today you have both been
mean to everyone!" said Grace.

Mrs. Jenkins sat down at the piano.
"Everybody stop and sing the
'Friendly' song!" she said.

Everybody sang,

"Be my pal.

See me smile!

Wear my shoes

And walk a mile.

Hold my hand

Be my friend.

And we'll never never never never

never NEVER fight again!"

The Franks picked each other.

Everybody square-danced.

And Mrs. Jenkins's bubble-gum

radar didn't beep once.

Dear Parents,

When our children were young we lived in a small house, but we always made a space just for books. When their dad or I would read a story out loud, the TV was always off—radio and music, too—because it intruded.

Soon this peaceful half hour of every day became like a little island vacation. Our children are lifetime readers now with an endless curiosity for the rich world waiting between the covers of good books. It cost us nothing but time well spent and a library card.

This set of easy-to-read books is about the real nitty-gritty of elementary school. There are new friends, and bullies, too. There are germs and the "Clean Hands" song, new ways of painting pictures, learning music, telling the truth, gossiping, teasing, laughing, crying, separating from Mama, scary Halloweens, and secret valentines. The stories are all drawn from the experiences my children had in school.

It's my hope that these books will transport you and your children to a setting that's familiar, yet new. And that it will prove to be a place where you can explore the exciting new world of school together.

Rosemary Wells